Dua Before Studying!

للَّهُمَّ انْفَعْنِي بِمَا عَلَّمْتَنِي وَ عَلِّمْنِي مَا يَنْفَعُنِي

اللَّهُمَّ إِنِّي أَسْأَلُكَ فَهْمَ النَّبِيِّينَ وَ حِفْظَ الْمُرْسَلِينَ الْمُقَرَّبِينَ.

اللَّهُمَّ اجْعَلْ لِسَانِي عَامِرًا بِذِكْرِكَ وَ قَلْبِي بِخَشْيَتِكَ. .

.إِنَّكَ عَلَى مَا تَشَاءُ قَدِيرُ وَ أَنْتَ حَسْبُنَا اللهُ وَ نِعْمَ الْوَكِيلُ

"ALLAHUMMA INFA'NII BIMAA 'ALLAMTANII WA'ALLIMNII MAA YANFA'UUNII.

ALLAHUMMA INII AS'ALUKA FAHMAL-NABIYYEN WA HIFZAL MURSALEEN AL-MUQARRABEEN.

ALLAHUMMA IJAL LEESANEE 'AIMAN BI DHIKRIKA WA QALBI BI KHASHYATIKA.

INNAKA 'ALA MA-TASHA'U QADEER WA ANTA HASBUN-ALLAHU WA NA'MAL WAKEEL."

OH ALLAH!
MAKE USEFUL FOR ME THAT WHAT YOU HAVE TAUGHT ME AND TEACH ME
KNOWLEDGE THAT WILL BE USEFUL TO ME.

OH ALLAH!
I ASK YOU FOR THE UNDERSTANDING OF THE PROPHETS AND THE
MEMORY OF THE MESSENGERS, AND THOSE NEAREST TO YOU.

OH ALLAH!
MAKE MY TONGUE FULL OF YOUR REMEMBRANCE AND MY HEART
WITH AWE OF YOU.

OH ALLAH!
YOU DO WHATEVER YOU WISH, AND YOU ARE MY AVAILER AND
PROTECTOR AND BEST OF AID.

ALLAH

The Only One God

Allah is the Unique Name of God.

The Being who is perfect in every way, in His knowledge, His power, His wisdom...

He is Allah, other than whom there is no deity, Knower of the unseen and the witnessed. He is the Entirely Merciful, the Especially Merciful.

What Does the Oneness of Allah's Names and Attributes Mean?

Oneness in attributes means that the qualities of the Almighty Allah are His very being and not additional to His being.

AL-GHAFOOR

The Great Forgiver

The All-Forgiving.
The One who forgives
immensely.

الغفور

Al-Ghafoor
The Exceedingly Forgiving

Ash-Shakoor

The Acknowledging One

The Grateful. The Appreciative.
The One who gives rewards
for a little obedience.

Ash-Shakoor

The Most Appreciative

Al-'Alee

The Sublime One

The Most High. The One who
is clear from attributes of
His creations.

Al-'Alee

The Most High, The Exalted

الْكَبِيرُ

Al-Kabeer

The Great One

The Most Great. The One who
is greater than everything
in existence.

Al-Kabeer

The Greatest, The Most Grand

Al-Hafeedh

The Guarding One

The Preserver. The Protector.
The One who protects whatever
and whoever He wills.

Al-Hafeedh
The Preserver

المُقِيت

Al-Muqeet

The Sustaining One

The Maintainer. The Guardian.
The Feeder. The One who has
the Power.

Al-Muqeet

The Sustainer

الحسيب

Al-Haseeb

The Reckoning One

The Reckoner. The One who knows in detail the account of things that people do throughout their lives.

Al-Haseeb

The Reckoner, The Sufficient

الجَلِيلُ

Al-Jaleel

The Majestic One

The Beneficent. The One who is
attrtibuted with greatness of
Power and Glory status.

Al-Jaleel

The Majestic

Al-Kareem

The Bountiful One

The Generous One. The Gracious.
The One who is continously giving
forth the grandest and most
precious bounty.

Al-Kareem

The Most Generous

Ar-Raqeeb

The All-Watchful

The Watcher. The One that
nothing is absent from Him.

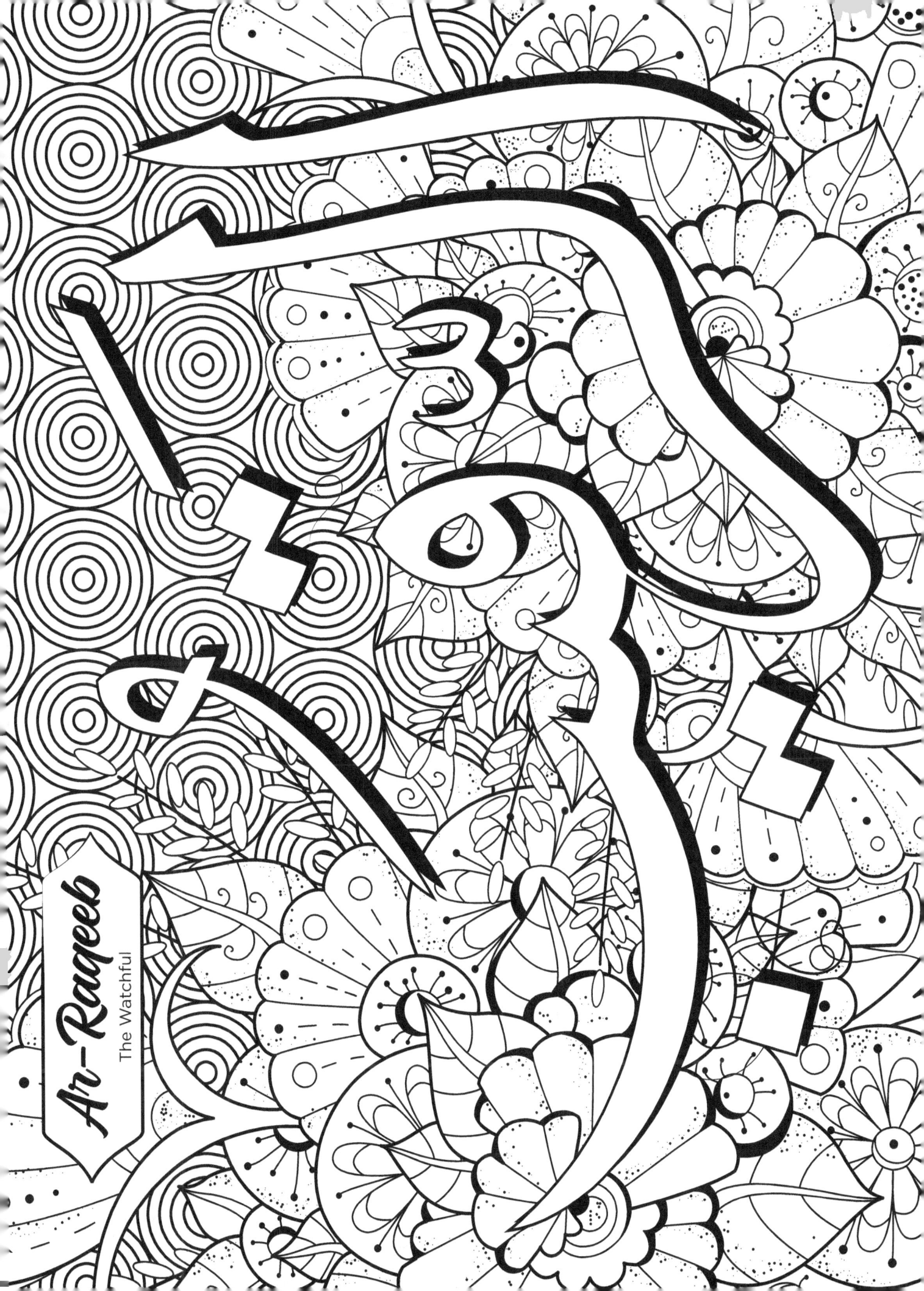

An-Raqeeb

The Watchful

Al-Mujeeb

The Responsive One

The Fulfiller of Prayers.
The One who responds to requests,
prayers and praise by means of
gifts and acceptance.

Al-Mujeeb
The Responsive One

Al-Wassi

The All-Encompassing

The Vast. The All-Embracing.
The One who has limitless
capacity and abundance.

Al-Wassi
The All-Encompassing

Al-Hakeem

The All-Wise

The One who has ultimate
wisdom. The One who is
correct in His creations.

Al-Hakeem
The All-Wise

الْوَدُودُ

Al-Wadood

The Most Loving

He who loves those who do
good and bestows on them
His compassion.

Al-Wadood

The Most Loving

Al-Majeed

The Glorious One

The One who is perfect in power.
High Status, Compassionate,
Generosity and Kindess.

Al-Majeed
The Glorious

الْبَاعِثُ

Al-Ba'ith

The Resurrector

The One who resurrects life to all creatures on the day of judgment.

Al-Bai''th
The Resurrector

Ash-Shaheed

The All-Observing

The Witness.
The One who nothing is
absent from Him.

Ash-Shaheed

The All- and Ever Witnessing

Al-Haqq
The Absolute Truth
The Truth. The True.
The One who truly exist.

Al-Haqq
The Absolute Truth

Al-Wakeel

The Disposer of Affairs

The Trustee. The One who
gives satisfaction and is
relied upon.

Al-Wakeel

The Disposer of Affairs

Al-Qawiyy

The Possessor of
All-Strength

The Most Strong.
The One with complete
and ultimate power.

Al-Qawiyy
The All-Strong

Al-Mateen

The Firm One

The One with exteme power which
is uninterrupted and He is not
restless or tired.

Al-Mateen

The Firm, The Steadfast

Al-Waliyy

The Protecting Associate

The Protecting Friend.
The Supporter.

Al-Waliyy
The Protecting Associate

Al-Hameed

The Praiseworthy.

The praised One who
deserves to be praised.

Al-Hameed

The Praiseworthy

Al-Muhsee
The All-Enumerating
The Counter. The Reckoner.
The One who the count of things
are known to Him.

Al-Muhsee
The All-Enumerating

Al-Mubdi

The Originator

The founder of creation.
The One who is the originator
of all His creations.

Al-Mubdi
The Originator

المُعِيدُ

Al-Mu'id

The Restorer

The Reproducer.
The One who brings back
the creatures after death.

Al-Mu'id

The Restorer

المُحْيِي

Al-Muhyee

The Maintainer of Life

The Restorer. The Giver of Life.
The One who created humans
from a clot of blood and breath
life into existance.

Al-Muhyee

The Giver of Life

Al-Mumeet

The Inflictor of Death

The Creator of Death.
The Destroyer. The One who
renders the living dead.

Al-Mumeet

The Bringer of Death

Al-Hayy
The Eternally Living

The Alive. He who is eternally
sound. The One Life from whom
all life arises.

Al-Hayy
The Ever-Living

Al-Qayyoom

The Self Subsiting One

He who holds the entire
universe. He who is free of any
dependance of anything
else for existance.

Al-Qayyoom

The Sustainer

Al-Waajid

The All-Perceiving

The Rich who is never poor.
The One who perceives and
possess everything. The One
who has no wants and
who lacks nothing.

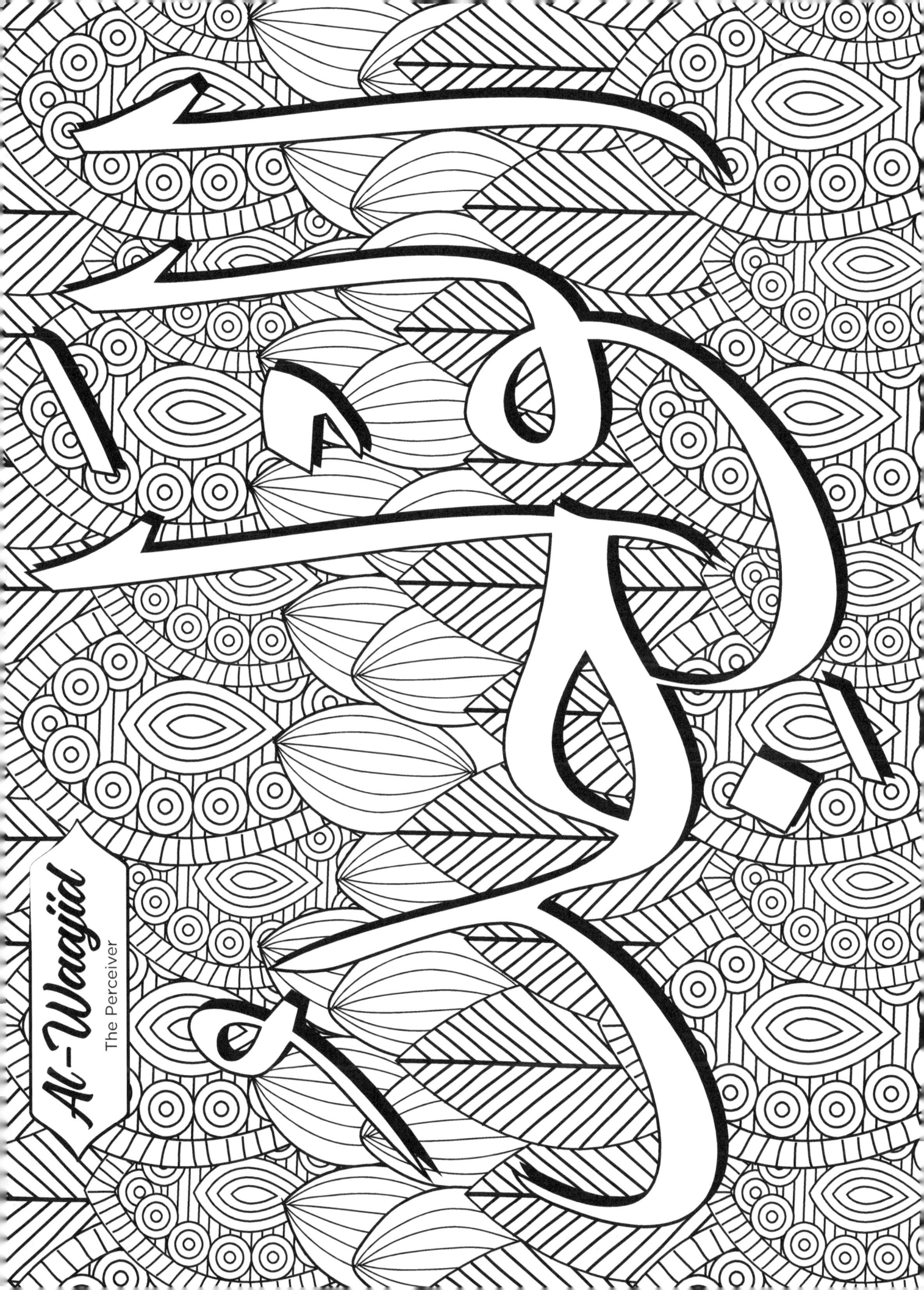

Al-Waajid

The Perceiver

Al-Maajid

The All-Noble One

The Glorious. The Most Noble.
The One whose deeds are
dignified, honorable &
exceedingly generous.

Al-Maajid

The Magnificent

الوَاحِد

Al-Waahid

The Unique
The One without partner or
equal in His attributes.

Al-Waahid

The One Who is Unique

Dua After Studying

اللَّهُمَّ إِنِّي أَسْتَوْدِعُكَ مَا قَرَأْتُ وَمَا حَفَظْتُ، فَرُضْهُ عَلَيَّ عِنْدَ حَاجَتِي إِلَيْهِ، إِنَّكَ عَلَى مَا تَشَاءُ قَدِيرٌ وَأَنْتَ حَسْبِي وَنِعْمَ الوَكِيل

ALLAHUMMA INNI ASTAODEEKA MA QARA'TU WAMA HAFAZ-TU. FARUDDUHU 'ALLAYA

INDA HAJATI ELAHI. INNAKA 'ALA MA-TASHA'-U QADEER WA ANTA HASBEEYA

WA NA'MAL WAKEEL.

OH ALLAH!

MAKE USEFUL FOR ME WHAT YOU HAVE TAUGHT ME AND TEACH
ME KNOWLEDGE THAT WILL BE USEFUL TO ME.

OH ALLAH!

I ENTRUST YOU WITH WHAT I HAVE READ AND I HAVE STUDIED.

OH ALLAH!

BRING IT BACK TO ME WHEN I AM IN NEED OF IT.

OH ALLAH!

YOU DO WHATEVER YOU WISH, YOU ARE MY AVAILER AND
PROTECTOR AND THE BEST OF AID.

The 99 Attributes of Allah coloring book series will motivate you to learn, memorize and understand the meaning of Allah's attributes. The second volume contains 33 unique and beautiful names along with a variety of ornate and detailed illustrations.

There are many health benefits of adult coloring books. For example, it can reduce stress, decrease anxiety, improve motor skills, improve sleep, helps you focus and relaxes the brain.
Coloring goes beyond being a fun activity for relaxation!

We hope you find enjoyment and benefit in our coloring book series.
Make sure to share them with your family and friends.

COLLECT ALL 3 VOLUMES!

Visit us at **mugirls.com** for other
coloring book series.

mugirls.com